REA

FRIENDS
OF ACPL

P9-EGN-147

362.
Tayl
The

DO NOT REMOVE
CARDS FROM POCKET

ALLEN COUNTY PUBLIC LIBRARY

FORT WAYNE, INDIANA 46802

You may return this book to any agency, branch,
or bookmobile of the Allen County Public Library.

DEMCO

Allen County Public Library
900 Webster Street
PO Box 2270
Fort Wayne, IN 46801-2270

To Bob who always needs a hand
and to Nicholas who always wants to give one. — CT

To my family, to my father. — JTD

This book owes much to Jim Robertson and Victoria Rock, and to
Lael Robertson for her marvelous designs. The author thanks the Tuohys
C.M.A., Hobart and Anne for their love and support. - CT
Text copyright © 1992 by Clark Taylor
Illustrations copyright © 1992 by Jan Thompson Dicks
All rights reserved.
Book design by Lael Robertson
The publisher extends very special thanks to South Sea International
Press, Ltd. for donating a portion of the prepress and printing
services to help make this book a reality.

Taylor, Clark (J. Clark)
The house that crack built / by Clark Taylor; illustrated by Jan Thompson Dicks.
Summary: Cumulative verses describe the creation, distribution,
and destructive effects of crack cocaine.
ISBN 0-8118-0133-0. — ISBN 0-8118-0123-3 (pbk.)
1. Crack (Drug) — United States — Juvenile poetry.
[1. Crack (Drug) 2. Cocaine. 3. Drug abuse.]
I. Dicks, Jan Thompson, ill. II. Title.
HV5809.5.T39 1992
362.29'8 — dc20   91-29651
                                                   CIP
                                                   AC

Printed in Hong Kong.

Distributed in Canada by Raincoast Books
112 East Third Avenue, Vancouver B.C. V5T 1C8
10 9 8 7 6 5 4 3

Chronicle Books
275 Fifth Street
San Francisco, California 94103

The House That Crack Built

Written by CLARK TAYLOR ▼ Illustrated by JAN THOMPSON DICKS
Afterword by MICHAEL PRITCHARD

Chronicle Books ▼ San Francisco

This is the House that crack built.

This is the Man

▼

who lives in the House that crack built.

These are the Soldiers who guard the Man

▼

who lives in the House that crack built.

These are the Farmers who work in the heat

▼

and fear the Soldiers who guard the Man

who lives in the House that crack built.

These are the Plants that people can't eat,

▼

raised by the Farmers who work in the heat
and fear the Soldiers who guard the Man
who lives in the House that crack built.

3 1833 02129 7897

This is the Drug known as cocaine,

▼

made from the Plants that people can't eat,
raised by the Farmers who work in the heat
and fear the Soldiers who guard the Man
who lives in the House that crack built.

This is the Street of a town in pain

▼

that cries for the Drug known as cocaine,
made from the Plants that people can't eat,
raised by the Farmers who work in the heat
and fear the Soldiers who guard the Man
who lives in the House that crack built.

This is the Gang, fleet and elite,

▼

that rules the Street of a town in pain
that cries for the Drug known as cocaine,
made from the Plants that people can't eat,
raised by the Farmers who work in the heat
and fear the Soldiers who guard the Man
who lives in the House that crack built.

This is the Cop working his beat

▼

who battles the Gang, fleet and elite,
that rules the Street of a town in pain
that cries for the Drug known as cocaine,
made from the Plants that people can't eat,
raised by the Farmers who work in the heat
and fear the Soldiers who guard the Man
who lives in the House that crack built.

This is the Boy feeling the heat,

▼

chased by the Cop working his beat
who battles the Gang, fleet and elite,
that rules the Street of a town in pain
that cries for the Drug known as cocaine,
made from the Plants that people can't eat,
raised by the Farmers who work in the heat
and fear the Soldiers who guard the Man
who lives in the House that crack built.

And this is the Crack that numbs the pain,

▼

bought from the Boy feeling the heat,

chased by the Cop working his beat

who battles the Gang, fleet and elite,

that rules the Street of a town in pain

that cries for the Drug known as cocaine,

made from the Plants that people can't eat,

raised by the Farmers who work in the heat

and fear the Soldiers who guard the Man

who lives in the House that crack built.

This is the Girl who's killing her brain,

▼

smoking the Crack that numbs the pain,
bought from the Boy feeling the heat,
chased by the Cop working his beat
who battles the Gang, fleet and elite,
that rules the Street of a town in pain
that cries for the Drug known as cocaine,
made from the Plants that people can't eat,
raised by the Farmers who work in the heat
and fear the Soldiers who guard the Man
who lives in the House that crack built.

And this is the Baby with nothing to eat,

▼

born of the Girl who's killing her brain,
smoking the Crack that numbs the pain,
bought from the Boy feeling the heat,
chased by the Cop working his beat
who battles the Gang, fleet and elite,
that rules the Street of a town in pain
that cries for the Drug known as cocaine,
made from the Plants that people can't eat,
raised by the Farmers who work in the heat
and fear the Soldiers who guard the Man
who lives in the House that crack built.

And these are the Tears we cry in our sleep

▼

that fall for the Baby with nothing to eat,
born of the Girl who's killing her brain,
smoking the Crack that numbs the pain,
bought from the Boy feeling the heat,
chased by the Cop working his beat
who battles the Gang, fleet and elite,
that rules the Street of a town in pain
that cries for the Drug known as cocaine,
made from the Plants that people can't eat,
raised by the Farmers who work in the heat
and fear the Soldiers who guard the Man
who lives in the House that crack built.

Afterword

This is a book about choices. Not just the choice of saying yes or no to drugs, but the choices that each of us makes every day. There has been a great deal of focus on teaching our children to say no to drugs, yet time has shown that we must give our children more than the right words. We must give them lives filled with opportunity. We must give them hope for the future. For where there is no hope, there is no choice.

It is easy to say that we, as ordinary people, can not effect the changes necessary to insure that all our children have full and healthy lives. That is the choice we make. We can either choose to ignore the issue, lamenting that it is too big for us to solve, or we can do what we can to make the world a better place. We can either decide it is someone else's problem or we can choose to face the problem as our own. As parents, grandparents, brothers, sisters, friends, neighbors and educators, we make these choices every time we decide what we teach our children, who we vote for, what jobs we take, what we do with our money and what we do with our time.

The people who created this book faced the same choices. And they chose to do what they could with their talents and time to confront this issue. The author used his poetic voice to remind us that the problem is out there. The illustrator used her artistic vision to bring the tragic nature of the problem powerfully alive. And the publisher chose to blend these visions into a book and to use its profits from that book to help fight the problem. Together, they have created a tool that can be used to open up discussion and to help children learn to make the right choices. Together they have reminded us that in small and personal ways each of us has the power to change the world.

—Michael Pritchard

For Further Information or Help

▼

If you or someone you know needs help with a drug problem, do something about it now. If you would like information to educate your children about the dangers of drug abuse, do something about it now. If you would like to contribute time and/or money to help fight this growing problem, do something about it now.

Across the country there are organizations that can provide help for and education about drug abuse. Local organizations can be found by looking in the yellow pages of the phone book—under "drug"—or by calling the local department of public health services, city hall, hospitals, doctors, or church or temple.

The following organizations have nationwide networks. Most of them have toll-free numbers that can be called for information and local referrals.

1. National Council on Alcoholism and Drug Dependents
1-800-NCA-CALL (1-800-622-2255)

The NCA can provide referral to drug and alcohol service organizations at the state and community levels.

2. American Council for Drug Education
1-800-488-3784
204 Monroe Street, Suite 110
Rockville, MD 20850

ACDE works to prevent drug abuse through public education. The Council assists educators, parents and community leaders in their efforts to address drug abuse and produces materials to help prevent drug abuse by high-risk groups, including adolescents, young working adults, women of childbearing age, and the elderly.

3. PRIDE
1-800-241-7946
(404) 658-2548
Suite 1216, 100 Edgewood Avenue
Atlanta, Georgia 30303

PRIDE is a resource information and training organization for communities concerned with adolescent drug abuse. It distributes accurate health information and provides parent and youth networks.

4. National Association for Perinatal Addiction Research and Education
1-800-638-BABY—crack/cocaine baby help line
312-329-2512
11 East Hubbard Street, Suite 200
Chicago, IL 60611

NAPARE provides treatment programs for pregnant, substance-abusing women and their children on an in and outpatient basis. NAPARE provides research and education materials for professionals working in drug treatment programs for women. The baby help line is open for questions and concerns.

5. The United Way of America

The United Way provides a full spectrum of services—including substance abuse prevention and rehabilitation. Look in the yellow pages of your phone book—under "U"—for local affiliates.

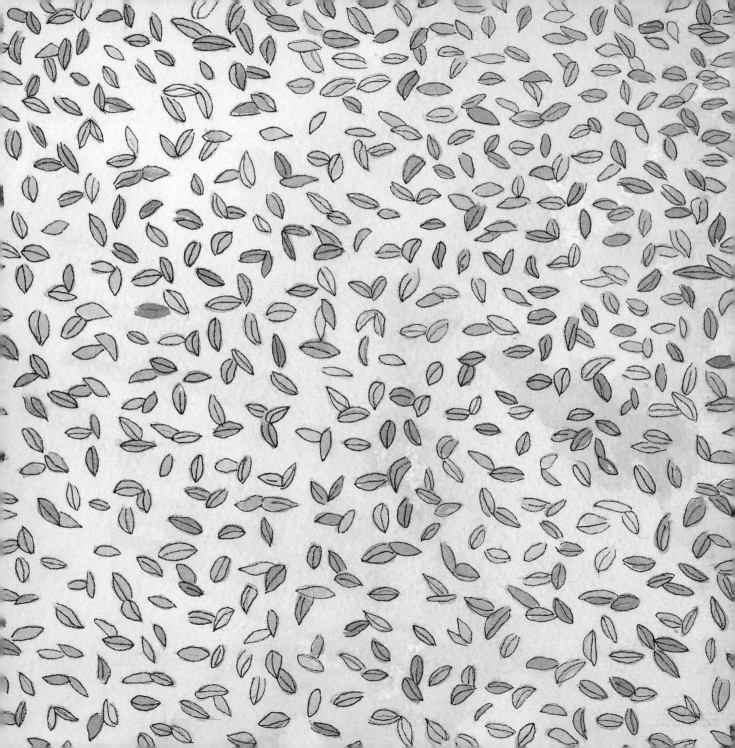